NEW
YOU
FOR
EVER

# NEW YOU FOR EVER

## STEVE COLE

Illustrated by
Chris King

Barrington Stoke

Published by Barrington Stoke
An imprint of HarperCollins*Publishers*
1 Robroyston Gate, Glasgow, G33 1JN

www.barringtonstoke.co.uk

HarperCollins*Publishers*
Macken House, 39/40 Mayor Street Upper,
Dublin 1, DO1 C9W8, Ireland

First published in 2026

Text © 2026 Steve Cole
Illustrations © 2026 Chris King
Cover design © 2026 HarperCollins*Publishers* Limited

The moral right of Steve Cole and Chris King to be identified
as the author and illustrator of this work has been asserted in accordance
with the Copyright, Designs and Patents Act, 1988

ISBN 978-0-00-873537-1

10 9 8 7 6 5 4 3 2 1

All rights reserved. No part of this publication may be reproduced, stored in a retrieval system, or transmitted, in whole or in any part in any form or by any means, electronic, mechanical, photocopying, recording or otherwise without the prior permission in writing of the publisher and copyright owners

Without limiting the exclusive rights of any author, contributor or the publisher of this publication, any unauthorised use of this publication to train generative artificial intelligence (AI) technologies is expressly prohibited. HarperCollins also exercise their rights under Article 4(3) of the Digital Single Market Directive 2019/790 and expressly reserve this publication from the text and data mining exception

A catalogue record for this book is available from the British Library

Printed and bound in India by Replika Press Pvt. Ltd.

This book contains FSC™ certified paper and other controlled
sources to ensure responsible forest management.

For more information visit: www.harpercollins.co.uk/green

*For Saskia*

# CONTENTS

01  Save the World by Living For Ever!   1

02  Hopes, Dreams and Data   4

03  Selfless   10

04  Perfect   14

05  The Right Ones   19

06  Cast Off   26

07  Happy Moments   30

08  A Band-Aid on a Burn   35

09  Truth and Power   41

10  Party Crash   45

| | | |
|---|---|---|
| 11 | Interview with a Pleeka | 53 |
| 12 | Hell of a Story | 60 |
| 13 | You Can't Go Home Again | 66 |
| 14 | They Know | 73 |
| 15 | Forced Exit | 79 |
| 16 | Waking Up | 85 |
| 17 | Gamble | 91 |
| 18 | Switch | 98 |
| 19 | Break-In Point | 105 |
| 20 | Ghost in the Machine | 111 |
| 21 | Age Is Just a Number | 121 |

This story
takes place
in the year
2070.

But it could
happen
sooner than
you think.

# CHAPTER 01

## Save the World by Living For Ever!

You see the chapter title above? It's bold, huh? Makes you want to find out more. Draws you into the story. Right?

I really hope you're nodding right now. Cos my job is to make a story sound good.

Even a wild and scary story like this one.

My name is Anders Jones. I'm not super-smart or anything, so I was kicked out of school at fourteen to help my dad with his TV news show, *And Finally*.

*And Finally* is a big show that goes out twice a week. I help Dad think of all the ideas and help set up the video shoots.

Together, we've made *And Finally* a big success. It's won Best Factual Presentation for the last two years. Probably because it's the only show offering a bit of *good* news. Dad and I try to show that happy stuff *can* happen. That there are reasons to be hopeful.

Enough reasons to fill a five-minute show twice a week in any case.

A lot of major TV channels run *And Finally* at the end of their main news bulletin each Friday and Sunday. It's like the news is a grim meal that tastes bad, and *our* show is a sweet treat you get after. It's meant to leave a happy taste in your mouth.

Last week, we shot a piece about the floodwater around St Paul's Cathedral, which is home to a newt everyone thought was extinct. The week before, we interviewed a woman who's raised the only remaining Scottish wildcats. That was one of my favourites. Those wildcat kittens were so cute!

But this week, my dad says the show needs to be about Pleekas again. This is weird cos we've covered Pleekas five times in the last three months.

"You have to understand, Anders," Dad told me. "I was born in the 2020s. Back then, Artificial Intelligence was everywhere. Code that could think for itself. But the code couldn't *feel* anything until we got the hang of Artificial *Emotional* Intelligence a bit later. And that changed everything."

Dad's right. It *did* change everything. It made Pleekas possible.

But what *are* Pleekas?

Read on. I'll fill you in.

# CHAPTER 02

## Hopes, Dreams and Data

The name "Pleeka" comes from the word "Replicas". Well, it does if you say it funny.

*Reh-PLEE-kuhs*.

I should write it Pleeka™ really, cos it's a trademark of the New You Foundation. But I won't cos it would get annoying.

Pleekas have been around for almost twenty years now. I guess the idea of replica people made sense – rather than fill a person with artificial organs bit by bit, their mind is put into an artificial body instead.

That's what a Pleeka is. An artificial body made of fake flesh that looks just like the old you. Or you pay extra to look better than you did! Apparently, the body feels like the old you too, only in peak condition – all the time.

If you had the desire – and the money – you could transform yourself. Like a puny caterpillar turning into an eternal, beautiful butterfly.

How?

First, your face and body are scanned. Every dimension, detail and colour are recorded so they can be duplicated in bio-plastic. Then nanobots – microscopic robots – are injected into your brainstem. They clone your memories and copy your personality. After that, the New You Foundation upload them to this artificial Pleeka body.

Pleekas never get sick. Never get tired. Never age. They survive injuries that would kill someone made of flesh and blood.

Pleekas don't need food or drink or exercise any more. But you can buy apps that give them thirst and hunger, and download special digital "eat-drinks" that satisfy those needs.

Pleekas don't need to sleep. All those hours in bed are a thing of the past, and so are trips to the toilet. No more flushing away your waste so

many times a day. No more wiping your bum! And Pleeka skin is anti-bacterial and doesn't sweat, meaning no more showering. All that water saved!

But human urges and emotions don't go away. Pleekas can still fancy people. If they fancy the Pleeka back, they can still do something about it. If they don't, the Pleeka can just switch off the heartache. As the Pleeka slogans say: *It's the full human experience but with none of the boring bits!*

*

The first Pleekas were made for old, sick, rich people who wanted strong, young bodies again. Their minds were put inside New You artificial bodies to be preserved for always. A bit like pickled onions in a jar of vinegar.

That was the idea anyway.

But there were problems with those early Pleekas. A lot of the artificial bodies broke down or went haywire. But people still took the risk cos they were going to die anyway. And as each new problem was solved, the next generation of Pleekas became safer and more reliable.

It made me think about my mum.

She died when I was just a little kid. She was a journalist like Dad. The two of them were covering the Great Water War of 2064, and Mum was drowned in the final assault on the Panama Canal. The northern locks were blown up, and she was swept away into the Caribbean Sea.

If she'd been a Pleeka, she would've survived. Pleekas don't breathe, so they can't drown.

Mum would have come back to us.

But it would never have happened. Mum was one of the millions who had protested *against* Pleekas. "Robots cosplaying as humans," she called them. Mum said they made a mockery of the human experience. "Just because you *can* do something, it doesn't mean you *should*. Who would turn their hopes, dreams and secrets into data?"

The answer was: lots of people.

Not just the old folk. There were people who'd been badly injured in accidents or who had terminal illnesses. And others who just found real life dull compared to "going digital".

*Pop inside a Pleeka!* the adverts told them. *Get the life you're owed!*

Of course, the people who became Pleekas soon owed the New You Foundation a shedload of cash cos they had to pay for their Pleeka batteries to be replaced every year.  Mum was right not to like them back then.

Today, things are different.  Pleeka batteries only need changing every eighty years.

The New You Foundation says that Pleekas can go on for ever.

# CHAPTER 03

## Selfless

The first story Dad and I did about Pleekas was kind of silly. There was this birdwatcher who hadn't seen a bird for months. There aren't many birds left these days. He felt so strongly about what was being lost in the world that he chose to turn Pleeka. That way, he could stand completely still for hours, like a statue. It worked! Occasionally, a raggedy old pigeon came and perched on him.

The second *And Finally* story on Pleekas was much better. This woman had been in a coma for years. Her family saved up, got her mind scanned and transplanted it into a Pleeka version. The Pleeka woke up straight away. It meant the woman was back with her kids and her partner. A nice story.

I heard that Pleeka sales shot up after that.

But not everyone thought it was the answer. There was this nineteen-year-old boy with a really bad illness. Doctors said they could make him Pleeka, but his parents refused. They thought it was unnatural. It was their decision, but the whole world had something to say about it, either agreeing or disagreeing with them.

Amazingly, the boy survived his illness in the end. "Miracles happen," said his mum.

"With Pleekas, they don't have to," the New You Foundation said.

And a lot of people listened.

There was this great firefighter who'd saved loads of lives in the California wildfires. He was supposed to retire, but instead he turned himself Pleeka so he could go on saving people in trouble. Imagine being so selfless you become a totally *different* self!

Last year, the New You Foundation started offering big discounts on Pleekas. You could buy one for less than the price of a car.

Not long after, a group of physics students chose to turn Pleeka in their early twenties! They said they did it so they could stop using up resources such as food and water. They felt they owed it to the planet. They called for other students to follow their example and take the strain off Earth.

After those students, more and more influencers jumped on the bandwagon to promote Pleekas. Not just as a cure for the sick and old but as a life choice.

Before long, celebrities came on board, including all four members of a big K-Pop band called Monsta-X.

That's right – the entire band has turned Pleeka. And these guys are only a few years older than me, eighteen or nineteen. They are the youngest Pleekas ever.

Today, Dad and I have come to a special venue in London for the launch of the new Monsta-X album, *MIND-SOUL HERO*. It's also to promote the next generation of Pleeka, the series 3000s.

Dad and I are waiting with the other news crews for the launch to kick off in the fancy hotel lounge. I'm looking at the 3D poster of the band in front of us.

"I've heard of manufactured pop bands before, but this is ridiculous," Dad says.

"It's happening though," I say. The virtual band members stare back at me from the poster as if they know I'm there. "It's really happening."

It feels like I'm looking into the future with eyes that belong to the past.

# CHAPTER 04

## Perfect

It's almost launch time. I can hear the excited screams and cries of an army of Monsta-X fans outside. We've been told that two hundred people will be watching in the "fan paddock" below the press room. Two hundred! I can't imagine so many people squashed in together. The government don't usually allow gatherings of that size.

I guess the New You Foundation has friends in high places.

"Live events in front of an audience used to happen all the time when I was young," Dad says fondly. "Thousands of people would turn up to football games each week—"

"And you had to stay at school cos AIs weren't doing all the jobs back then, blah, blah ..." I fake yawn in Dad's direction. "You might just have mentioned this stuff, like, a zillion times ..."

"Never mind school, Anders," Dad says. "I'm just saying football was better when it wasn't virtual. You know, when there were real audiences."

"Everyone squashed up together in the rain, spreading viruses?" I shudder. "I'm glad big crowds were banned."

Dad just shakes his head. It's funny to think how different the world was for him, growing up in the 2020s. Back then, climate change was a big deal, but there was still hope that the world could be fixed. As Dad grew up, those hopes slipped away because fixing it cost too much, and no one was prepared to pay.

I guess we all paid in the end.

The world warmed up and the oceans rose, meaning the only weather was extreme weather. Cities flooded and villages blew away. Crops were ruined, either submerged or scorched. Farm animals didn't have enough grass to graze on. And rivers and lakes dried up or became too polluted to use.

That led to a shortage of food and water. Not just here in the UK but all around the world. This is why we all eat crickets for protein these days. I've seen pictures online of actual cows and sheep and pigs, before all the farms were built over cos we needed the land for houses. Those things look so cute! How did anyone ever eat them?

Well, Dad used to, when he was little. He became a TV broadcaster because he wanted to educate people about all the stuff that was going wrong in the world. He hoped that together people could make things better. But Dad doesn't preach at people. That turns people off. Instead, he tries to make them smile and think about how things could be better if we all had more things to smile about.

*

The double doors at the far end of the room open, and a woman in a smart suit appears. She smiles, her teeth brilliant white between her crimson lips. "Ladies and gentlemen, I'm Mona Chen, President of the New You Foundation," she says.

"Please enter the hall, where Monsta-X will soon be performing."

"Can we talk to them?" Dad asks.

"Absolutely, Daniel," says Mona. "There will be a short Q and A after the performance."

I'm impressed. The woman in charge of New You knows Dad's name!

"The future is this way," Mona says, waving us into the hall. "You'll be seeing up close how PleekaLife is the best life."

Mona's smile grows wider. Her white teeth are perfect.

I get the feeling that everything is perfect in her world.

# CHAPTER 05

## The Right Ones

It's weird, watching the band perform. Knowing they aren't human like me and Dad and the others in the room is kind of unnerving.

But fair play to them. Monsta-X perform even better than I've seen online. They leap about in the light show and turn somersaults as they sing, all with perfect timing.

The screams of hysterical fans almost drown them out. It's also weird watching so many people whooping and whistling and singing along in the space below the press gallery. I've never seen so many people all squashed up together. I'm glad they're a safe distance away. Just imagining the sweaty smell turns my stomach.

When the performance is finished, Mona Chen invites Monsta-X to the front of the stage, and the crowd applaud wildly. I'm looking for ways to tell the band aren't human any more, but it's not easy. The Pleekas I've met in the past looked a bit stiff and waxy, you know? But these Monsta-X boys move smoothly and easily.

They're not out of breath, of course. Their chests rise and fall to give the impression of breathing, but Pleekas don't need to breathe. They're not sweating either.

They look almost like mannequins, but then I guess they always did.

Mona addresses the press gallery. "Now we have time for some questions from our friends in the media ..."

I raise my hand. A virtual microphone floats over and amplifies my voice. "Did you have to learn that amazing dance routine?" I ask. "Or is it programmed into your new bodies?"

"We worked it all out ourselves," says Jin, their lead singer. "But anyone who buys a Pleeka 3000 in the next thirty days gets the Monsta-X Moves app built in as standard!"

Mona nods eagerly, adding, "You can watch the routine, then dance it yourself perfectly – no practice or patience required!"

The fans whoop and cheer with excitement. I imagine myself up on stage leaping about like that without needing to practise beforehand. I have to admit, it does sound a pretty cool shortcut.

Someone at the back of the press gallery says, "I've interviewed you before and you spoke no English then."

"Pleeka 3000s come bundled with ten different languages as standard," says Mona Chen. "It's part of our 'Think It to Speak it' programme."

"Do your singing voices come out already autotuned?" another journalist asks to some laughter.

"Our vocal cords were cloned from the originals," Jin explains. He winks. "It's the same old us, just even more perfect than before."

There's applause, until a woman behind me asks, "How much were you paid to throw away your real bodies and become robots?"

The bandmates go silent.

"This is a partnership," says Mona Chen. Her eyes look like they might fire lasers at the woman. "These young men simply wished to do their bit to help the planet."

"How long will your Pleeka batteries last?" the woman persists. "You say at least eighty years before they need to be replaced. But the science doesn't agree. And what about the recent reports that say manufacturing a single Pleeka does more damage to the environment than a hundred human beings could do in a lifetime—"

"These claims are ridiculous," Mona interrupts. "And I can assure you, this so-called research will be disproven by a celebrity expert at the G12 Eco-Rally next week." Mona pauses for effect. "The expert is none other than Tera Helstrom."

There's applause from the fans below at the news, and I clap too. Tera Helstrom is only seventeen, but she's famous worldwide for telling the people in power what they're getting wrong when it comes to climate change.

With everything that's happened over the last fifty years, you'd think they'd be ready to listen. Rising sea levels swallowed miles of coastland from Norfolk to Lincolnshire, yet the politicians didn't seem to care much. It was only when the Thames finally broke its banks and Kensington and Chelsea were lost to the floods that an emergency government replaced the old one and took control.

That was fifteen years ago, and they're still in power now cos they voted to cancel elections until the climate emergency was over. Of course, it may never be over, so we're stuck with them. And a lot of people think they care more about making money for themselves than making things better.

So we need people like Tera. She left school at fourteen like I did. The AI teachers ruled that further education was no use to lower-ability kids. Only kids who excel in science and tech are encouraged to stay at school because the government says it's only them – the Big Thinkers – who can help shape our future.

I guess that Tera is to me what Greta Thunberg was to my dad growing up. Greta was a famous environmental activist. Tera gives a voice to us younger, ordinary people.

"Tera would never support this programme," the woman behind me shouts. "Get off me!"

I turn in time to see two huge men in dark suits grabbing the woman. Her big glasses nearly fall off her face as they march her out of the press gallery. I guess the New You Foundation don't want anyone spoiling the mood today.

The weird thing is, I'm sure that the woman is right. I remember watching a video where Tera was hating on Pleekas. She said a Pleeka helps the environment like a plaster helps a third-degree burn …

"I know that Tera's a big fan," says Jin with a big smile. "A fan of Monsta-X *and* Pleekas!" Jin holds out his arms to the crowd. "PleekaLife is great! You'll look better, work better, *be* better."

"That's right," Mona shouts over the whooping of the crowd. "And get this – the government has just announced that from next month the legal age for turning Pleeka will be lowered to sixteen!"

I turn to my dad, shocked. "Sixteen?" I mouth at him.

Dad doesn't look happy. He stares around us as the cheers of the young crowd grow deafening. It's as if they long to swap the bodies they were born into for something else.

# CHAPTER 06

## Cast Off

There's a party at the venue to celebrate the launch of the Pleeka 3000s and Monsta-X's new album.  But Jin and his bandmates don't stick around, and the sweaty fans are sent outside into the August cold.  The party is only for the press.

There are new Pleekas on display here.  They look eerily real.  The 3000 series models don't only come with batteries that last eighty years, deep discounts and interest-free credit.  They also have Realistic Pulse™, 200 AdvanceDance™ moves and a ForEver Makeover™ pack of cosmetic upgrades thrown in for free.  There are dozens of social media influencers here, cooing about how wonderful everything is.

But the woman with the glasses and the awkward questions doesn't come back.

*

On the way home, I wonder about Monsta-X as well. I can't believe how Jin and the rest of the band just ditched their healthy, human bodies like old clothes.

The law says that when someone turns into a Pleeka, their human form must be deep-frozen and kept in storage for up to three years in case of problems. After that, the body can be recycled – unless you pay a fortune to keep it. I've seen pictures online of high-tech storage, honeycombs that glitter with frost, each with somebody locked away inside.

Do those cold, human bodies dream of the life they've lost? Or are they dead in the dark, unaware of anything?

I find myself thinking of the Cloud. So much of my life is up there online somewhere in digital form: pictures and videos; songs and books. I don't own physical copies like Dad's parents used to, but so what? Digital is just as good.

So why shouldn't I go full real-artificial? I could have a battery in my chest instead of an old-fashioned heart. No more colds or catching a chill. And all the physical skills it takes normal people years to master can be bought and downloaded into a Pleeka body in a matter of minutes.

*

I think about that a lot over the next few weeks. Especially with the Pleeka adverts with Tera Helstrom voiceovers going viral on all channels.

"*Look at you,*" Tera says in the latest ad, smiling, her long red hair drifting about her face in slo-mo. "*You're fragile. Wondrous. Unique. You're too precious to be left to the random blows of Nature. And Nature is too precious to be left to the random blows of humanity.*"

Tera smiles. There's a bright blue planet Earth spinning in her palm.

"*Now there's a way you and Nature can enjoy a thriving future – with the new, improved Pleeka 3000 series.*" Tera breathes softly on the world in her hand, and it gently blows away, rising and shining in a fresh orbit. *"Being Pleeka won't cost as much as you think ... while being YOU will cost the Earth."*

And you know what?

These ads are making me feel like I'm not just *causing* pollution, but that I *am* the pollution.

Who wouldn't want to turn Pleeka?

# CHAPTER 07

## Happy Moments

Me and Dad usually hold our *And Finally* planning meetings on the last Sunday of every month. We check that upcoming shoots are prepared and kick around ideas for future shows.

Four weeks after the Monsta-X launch, I learn that Dad wants to make a whole bunch of shows about Pleekas.

"Our show is about happy moments around the world," Dad reminds me. "And while New You is a UK company, it's been expanding its business abroad too."

I scan Dad's list of stories on my float-screen. "Nineteen-year-old boy from Tibetan village who couldn't read or write wins competition to turn Pleeka with free Literacy Skills brain-pack ..."

"Three months later, he's teaching the other kids in his village how to read and write," Dad says.

"That's cool," I admit. "Sharing what he knows. But if the whole village turned Pleeka, they could download literacy skills in one go."

Dad nods. "Funny you should say that. New You has announced plans to sponsor similar villages around the globe to turn Pleeka. They're letting everyone be part of the future." Dad pushes another story to my float-screen. "And check this."

I read aloud: "Indonesian Pleekas explore the seabed at depths of almost two kilometres without protective gear ..."

"They've found the richest seam of cobalt and manganese in the North Pacific," Dad says, as proudly as if it's his own discovery. "New You have said they will give *And Finally* exclusive footage of the crew in action!"

I swipe the story away. "We don't have to go underwater, right?" I ask. "After what happened to Mum ..."

"We'll stay safe and dry, Anders," Dad says quietly. "Although they said this operation is also carrying out research into building a city on the seabed. If everyone lives for ever, they'll need to live somewhere ..."

"Hidden away under the ocean?" I shudder. "In all that pollution down there? And what happens when someone wants to visit – give them a wetsuit?"

"The city will be built inside a protective bubble," says Dad, rolling his eyes. "And the pollution will be pumped down into the bedrock. Neat and tidy."

"Tera Helstrom used to think that deep-sea mining was a bad thing," I remind him. "I know the coral reefs are all dead, but some fish populations are still—"

"The pros outweigh the cons," Dad interrupts me. "That's what Tera says now."

"Makes you wonder why she's changed her mind," I say.

Dad shrugs. "When the facts change, your opinions are allowed to change with them," he says.

"Ha! Depends who's changing the facts," I say.

Still, it seems that Dad's right. At the G12 Eco-Rally, Tera disproved each claim that Pleekas were bad for the environment – just like Mona Chen had predicted.

And an expert crusader like Tera would know the truth.

Wouldn't she?

Dad goes on. "Speaking of Tera Helstrom, you could be talking to her on Friday."

I blink. "Seriously?"

"You've heard of that girl who turned Pleeka on her sixteenth birthday?" Dad says.

"Sure. Youngest Pleeka on the planet, right? Cody someone."

"Cody Vempati." Dad nods with a grin. "She's the face of New You's Prima Pleeka youth range. Now the Pleeka age limit has been lowered to sixteen, they're launching a new press campaign."

I'm surprised. "They only just launched the Pleeka 3000 series."

"The youth market is worth billions," Dad says. "And Prima Pleekas come with free physical upgrades on your eighteenth and twenty-first birthdays. Mona Chen is inviting Cody to the New You Foundation's offices in London to decide the way she wants to look when she's eighteen and twenty-one. For maximum publicity, Monsta-X *and* Tera will be there to help Cody decide."

"And we shoot it all," I say, realising what Dad is telling me. I had been wondering what would happen to the youngest Pleekas. It would be weird if they stayed looking sixteen for ever, wouldn't it? And how cool to *choose* what you'll look like when you're older instead of settling for what Nature gives you!

Right?

# CHAPTER 08

## A Band-Aid on a Burn

It turned out that Dad couldn't shoot the underwater Pleeka piece. Nor could anyone else.

Apparently, there was an accident under the ocean. A sinkhole opened in the seabed and the deep-sea miners fell into it with all their equipment. They're still trapped in the water, buried under tons of rock.

Of course, the miners are Pleekas, so they aren't dead. They aren't even hurt. They don't need to breathe or eat or anything. They're just stuck down there in the dark until they're rescued.

"Mona says they're going to reschedule the shoot," Dad tells me after another planet-healthy dinner of crickets in glucose. "We won't lose the exclusive. But we're not allowed to say anything about the accident."

"Why not?" I ask him.

Dad hesitates. "Because if the news channels hear about it, the disaster becomes the story. And there goes our exclusive," he says.

It gets me thinking about my mum again. If she'd been a Pleeka, she could have survived the Panama Canal flooding. No problem.

"There's still the Cody Vempati piece to think about," Dad reminds me. "Mona thought that you could interview Cody, since you're about the same age."

I don't normally appear in front of the camera. That's Dad's job.

"I'd rather interview Tera Helstrom," I say. "Any chance?"

"We'll see." Dad looks thoughtful. "This Prima Pleeka launch is a big deal for New You. If enough sixteen-year-olds want to turn Pleeka, the government might lower the minimum age to fourteen."

"As young as that?" I frown. "Kids that age are still growing."

"And still using resources, still making waste ..." Dad says, shrugging. "Meeting the country's climate-change targets will be way easier with fewer people polluting and reproducing."

I think about it. It makes sense, I guess. At fourteen, the AI teachers decide who continues at school. Maybe they'll decide who gets to turn Pleeka too.

"Anyway," Dad says, getting up from his chair. "I'll call Mona about the Cody interview."

Dad goes off to his office to make the call. I've heard him talking to Mona pretty often lately. And I remember that Mona knew his name at the Monsta-X launch.

Ew – could Dad be into her or something?

But that's not the biggest question.

What I really want to know is what made Tera Helstrom change her mind about the New You Foundation and about Pleekas?

I decide to look online for the big speech she made against them.

But the video has vanished. I can't even find a mention of it anywhere.

I can't be imagining things. I wrote an essay about Tera in my final school exams, and I'm sure I quoted her speech.

*Bam!* I remember downloading the speech so I could quote from it offline. It'll be on my old device ...

I go to my bedroom. Dig out the tablet. Search for the speech.

Seconds later, I'm watching Tera Helstrom – a little younger and a whole lot angrier – streaming her speech to her followers online.

*"Pleekas help the environment as much as a Band-Aid helps a third-degree burn ... I say to the New You Foundation: how dare you expect me to sacrifice my right to live as flesh and blood, just so I fit your polluted vision of the future? Tech companies like yours could save the world. Instead, they want to save us to the Cloud and make us easier to manage! They could change their destructive, world-spoiling practices.*

*Instead, they want to change the concept of life itself. They're poisoning the planet for profit and creating a plastic population ..."*

"Whoa," I breathe. "You've really changed your tune, Tera Helstrom. What the hell happened to you?"

# CHAPTER 09

## Truth and Power

I hurry upstairs to Dad's office. I can't wait to see the look on his face when he hears this speech. But as I get closer, I can hear Dad, and I recognise Mona Chen's voice.

He's still on that call.

"The miners will all be back working the seabed by the seventeenth," she says.

"You've managed to rescue them!" Dad replies, sounding delighted. "What a story! It'll show people that Pleekas are the perfect workers for hazardous environments …"

"You misunderstand me, Daniel," says Mona. "Rescuing the miners is pointless. It's cheaper to download another copy of their digital mind-prints from our server and place them into new Pleeka bodies. They'll pick up the work where the last miners left off. Same difference."

I can't believe what I'm hearing. How can Mona be so heartless?

"But what about the first lot of miners who are trapped on the seabed?" asks Dad. "Will you shut them down remotely?"

"That would be murder," says Mona coldly. "Imagine the public outcry if we had the power to switch off our customers any time we chose. No, Dan, Pleekas have the same rights as any other human."

"But any other human would die and it would be over," says Dad. "Like … like my wife."

He stops talking for a few seconds. I close my eyes.

"Think of those poor people," Dad manages to continue. "They may not feel physical pain, but those Pleekas will spend every day trapped in the dark. With no hope. Unable to move. A living death—"

"Only for a year or so," says Mona. "Not even a Pleeka can withstand the pressures at those depths for too long." She pauses, then her voice grows harder. "Don't criticise our methods, Dan. You're being paid well to endorse the Pleekas."

I feel like my heart has got stuck in my throat. *This* is why we've been doing so many Pleeka stories – New You are paying us?

"Now, can we get back to the Prima Pleeka launch?" Mona says, calm again, as if nothing has happened. "When your son interviews Cody, we want him to say he's jealous of her turning Pleeka so young. As part of the country's happiest news show, he should encourage more young people to make the switch. He'll be boosting Pleeka sales. Saving the environment. Win-win."

My legs are trembling now at the thought they want to use me like this …

"If you let Anders think it's Tera Helstrom's idea, I think it'll work," Dad replies. "He'd do anything she asks him to."

"Good. Because Tera will do anything *I* ask her to," says Mona. "Arrive at the New You offices at 9 a.m. tomorrow. We'll have plenty of time to get things done before the main launch …"

Mona starts wrapping up the call, and I turn and duck away back down the stairs. *How could you, Dad?* I ask myself over and over.

And how could Tera be on board with New You when she used to hate Pleekas so much? What has she been promised?

Tomorrow, I won't be doing whatever I'm told.

Tomorrow, I'll find out the truth.

# CHAPTER 10

## Party Crash

The New You offices are fancy. The building is like a sprawling castle made of steel and concrete. It even has a garden outside and some actual flowers. Not the plastic versions – real growing grass and plants. Only the bees that pollinate them are artificial.

Dad and I are sitting in a self-drive cab, its nav systems steering us smoothly along a paved driveway. All the way here, I've stared out of the windows at grey roads and concrete and smog, dwelling on the stuff I overheard yesterday.

"Lawns are happy memories," Dad says. "I still remember when gardens were common. There were fields and meadows and all sorts, before we lost the bees—"

"I've heard this before," I say coldly. I'm in no mood for one of Dad's nostalgic stories of the olden days. After all, they led to the days we're stuck with now.

And all the days that lie ahead.

"You've been in a mood since yesterday," Dad complains. "What's wrong? I know last night's cricket curry wasn't the best dinner I ever made, but still ..."

Drones and workers – Pleeka workers probably – are building a stage in front of the main building. A bright pink convertible car is parked outside. It looks old. Like, maybe from the 2030s or something. It might even run on petrol! Only the richest of the rich can afford fossil fuels now.

"Expensive wheels," says Dad. "Who do you think came here in it – Monsta-X or Tera Helstrom?"

I force a smile at Dad and reply, "One way to find out."

We're greeted at the door by a junior assistant. She looks like a younger version of

Mona Chen. "Ah, Dan and Anders, right?" she says. "From *And Finally?*"

"Yes, we're here for the—" Dad starts to say.

He's cut off by a strangled shout from somewhere inside: "Help me!"

Two thoughts hit me – *Someone's in trouble* and *This could be news*. I feel a twinge of guilt cos I think the news one came first. Then I see Dad's already pulled out his camera ready to catch the action, and I know where I get my instincts from.

We duck past the assistant and run off down the corridor to where the shout came from.

In the middle of a big marble reception hall, there's a young man lying on the floor clutching his head. Two men in pale blue uniforms are holding him down while Mona Chen crouches beside him. Cody Vempati and her mother are to my left – I recognise them from Dad's file. They're dressed to party but look like they just watched a car crash.

I realise that the guy on the floor is Jin – the lead singer of Monsta-X.

"I want my body back!" Jin shouts. "Put me back in my body!"

Mona Chen looks up at me and Dad, and her face becomes a vicious snarl. "No cameras!" Mona shouts.

Jin suddenly shoves away the men holding him down. He springs to his feet, spins on his left leg and launches into a somersault. His face hits the marble with a horrible thump, but when he rolls over there's not a a mark on him. The two men in uniforms jump on him like wrestlers.

"It's not gonna work, you hear?" Jin moans. His head twitches like his neck is trying to shake it off. "I'm as stubborn as hell! It's not gonna work."

Mona Chen presses a large red disc to Jin's forehead. He shakes and goes limp. The two uniformed guys are still holding on to him as if not trusting him to stay that way, but Jin's eyes are closed, and his mouth hangs open.

For a moment, I think he's dead. Then I remember: this body was never really alive.

"He just came running downstairs and went wild," Cody says, wide-eyed. "Mum, that won't happen to me, will it?"

"Of course not, sweetheart," says Mrs Vempati, glaring around the room. "Not without a hell of a lot of legal action."

"What caused this to happen?" Dad asks. He points to the red disc in Mona Chen's hand. "What's that?"

Mona ignores Dad, gets up and turns to Cody's mum. Her smile looks automatic. "Please don't be alarmed," Mona says. "There's nothing to worry about. Jin was downloading the dance moves for this afternoon's show and disconnected before it was fully complete. This *can* upset the balance of brain and flesh."

Cody's mum gently removes herself from her daughter. "What made Jin stop?" she demands. "What's in your hand?"

"Just a tool. We call it a sleep-switch," Mona Chen tells her. "It safely powers down the brain into sleep mode. Jin will wake again soon and be fine."

"They did something similar with computers in the old days," Dad remarks. "It was called 'turning it off and on again'."

Jin stirs suddenly. He puts a hand to his head and starts speaking in Korean. Mona Chen smiles and talks back to him in his language.

"I'm not happy about this," Cody's mother announces. "I want a full explanation ..."

I wouldn't mind one either. But the next thing I know, the men in uniforms are ushering me and Dad and Cody and her mum to the lifts at the back of the hall. The assistant reappears and pretty much pushes us inside.

"It's time for the interview," the assistant says. "Cody, this is Anders and his father, Daniel, from *And Finally*."

"I love *And Finally*," says Cody.

Her mum nods. "We told New You that you were the only ones we wanted to talk to about this."

As the doors close and the lift glides upward, I get a closer look at Cody. She seems so ordinary. She's breathing like a real, live person. She's even swaying a little like a real, live person.

It's hard to believe that she's *not* a real, live person.

"That was so freaky downstairs just now," Cody says.

"You mean seeing Jin like that?" I ask.

"*Hearing* Jin like that," Cody corrects me. "Jin is Korean. When he had that funny turn, he was speaking in English. Then he woke up again speaking Korean."

"Auto-translate," Dad says. "Foreign languages come bundled with Pleeka 3000s, don't they?"

"*Si, señor*," Cody says with a nervous smile. "I know. I guess that was why. But it was still freaky."

The assistant says nothing. Her smile never comes near her eyes.

*Everything's freaky here*, I decide.

# CHAPTER 11

## Interview with a Pleeka

The assistant leads us into a sleek meeting room lit in pink and grey. Crickets in a variety of flavours lie on platters next to dispensers filled with vitamin water. No expense spared here!

The assistant shepherds me and Cody over to a virtual TV set: two chairs in front of a blank screen so the various networks can drop in their own logos behind us. There's a big virtual banner above it that reads: **PRIMA PLEEKA – AGE IS JUST A NUMBER**, with *16–18–21* written in bright pink.

The assistant taps her smart collar, and a float-screen bobs between us. "We've written out the questions we'd like you to ask," she tells me.

"But I've got my own questions," I protest.

The assistant keeps smiling. "These questions are pre-approved by Mona Chen."

I scan the words on the screen. Like Mona threatened, I'm really meant to say: "*Wow, I'm so jealous of you, Cody.*"

"No way," I say. "Dad, we don't work like this."

"We don't," Dad agrees. He moves for the door, looking unhappy. "Hold fire, Anders. I'll talk to Mona."

The assistant looks alarmed and hurries after Dad, leaving me with the float-screen. "Sir, she's busy—" the assistant calls to him.

"Then she'll have to make time," says Cody's mum firmly, following them out. "My daughter might be Pleeka, but she's not a performing puppet …"

I watch the door close after them. Bolts automatically slide shut, locking us in.

Cody's looking at me. Her eyes are perfect – blue and clear.

She shifts a little awkwardly and says, "You're staring."

"Sorry, I don't mean to," I tell her. "I guess I'm a bit shaken up after whatever happened to Jin down there."

"Same," says Cody. "Weird, wasn't it? Scary."

"Are you worried that something like that might happen to you?" I ask slowly.

"There are bound to be a few growing pains. Even if I've stopped growing." Cody laughs, a high-pitched tinkle. She sounds nervous. "But the pain I used to have …"

I nod. "I read the New You press release. You had fibromyalgia, right?"

"Yes. Burning pain all over my body, headaches, tired the whole time." Cody shrugs. "Now I'm Pleeka, it's like my soft tissues have been rinsed – along with Mum's wallet!"

Cody laughs, and I laugh too. I can see that PleekaLife does come with some advantages.

"Sounds like it wasn't a hard choice to turn Pleeka," I say.

"I've honestly never felt better," says Cody. "Some people resist new technology. Other people are early adopters. Guess at sixteen, I'm the earliest adopter around!" She laughs. "And Mona said that the high discounts New You are offering have really boosted Pleeka sales in the UK. Eight million people have signed up already."

"Really?" I frown. "That's, like, ten per cent of the UK population."

"Pretty sure," Cody says, tapping on her float-screen. "Let me download the latest figures in case I'm getting it all wrong." She laughs another little tinkling noise.

With a clunk, the bolts on the door slide open. The float-screen in front of me is glitching like it's broken. I hear Cody laugh again.

I turn to her, and her face is screwed up. It's like she's suddenly frozen.

"Cody?" I say, waving my hand in front of her face, but she doesn't blink. The laugh keeps coming from her, again and again.

Then Cody's face relaxes, and she stares at me. "It's not gonna work," she says. "It's not gonna work."

*That's what Jin was saying, I realise. And Cody was downloading something. Just like Jin was.*

I try to reboot Cody's float-screen to see if I can contact Dad, or the assistant, or anyone. But nothing's working. Something has happened to the tech in this place.

A systems crash?

Has it hit the whole building?

If it's strong enough to affect a Pleeka ...

Cody is still muttering over and over, "It's not gonna work."

What if something's really wrong? I run for the unlocked door and look in the corridor for help.

It's deserted.

I hurry to the lifts so I can get back to the reception hall. The lifts aren't working, so I take the door to the stairwell.

Big mistake.

I collide with someone running down the stairs. I can't see who because I'm already falling down, and long red hair is spilling over my face. I land on my back with a gasp. Then time seems to slow as I see icy grey eyes staring down at me from a face scattered with freckles.

Shocked, I stare up at her.

"You're Tera Helstrom," I whisper.

"That's right," she says. "And unless I get out of here, I'm dead."

# CHAPTER 12

## Hell of a Story

It's fair to say that I never expected to find a mega-celeb like Tera Helstrom sitting beside me in the back seat of an auto-cab. We're on the run.

I'm sweating, and my heart's racing. I'm expecting the car to stop at any moment and the police to swoop down on us like flies onto food.

Since running into Tera, everything's happened so fast.

After our collision, we took those stairs down to the ground floor, and she told me the New You Foundation were keeping her locked up. Forcing her to promote PleekaLife™. Just like that, all my suspicions were confirmed.

So I had to help Tera out, didn't I? In the moment, it seemed like the only right thing to do.

That weird system glitch that messed up Cody, the float-screen and the lifts also shut down the building's security systems. Maybe that's what affected Jin from Monsta-X too. The fire door at the bottom of the stairwell opened into the grounds without an alarm going off, and the security drones weren't flying but scattered over the lawn and concrete.

I'd been certain that someone would spot me and Tera from a window as I led her to the auto-cab me and Dad took to get here. Thank god the car wasn't affected by the glitch. Thank Dad for not locking down the controls.

Now I'm hugging myself in the back seat while Tera Helstrom just sits there. I'm weirded out by being so close to someone famous. Someone I looked up to.

I pour some water into the cap of my flask and offer it to Tera. She shakes her head, so I drink it myself.

"Thanks for getting me away," says Tera, rubbing the back of her head. "Who are you?

What were you even doing at the New You offices?"

"I'm Anders Jones. I was meant to be doing an interview for a news show," I tell her. "It's called *And Finally*."

"I know it," Tera says. "Sweet little stories to make people feel good while the planet burns. Let me guess: Mona Chen paid your dad a ton of money to give them good press."

I nod and reply, "She's definitely paying him something."

"See, this is what the New You Foundation bosses do. They use bribery to get what they want. And if they can't bribe someone, they threaten them instead."

I shrug. "If that's true," I say, "why has no one reported them to the police?"

"I'm sure people *have* reported them. But New You is above the law." Tera looks at me. "Mona Chen forced me to become a Pleeka spokesperson. If I refused, she said she'd buy up the last wetlands and conservation areas and build factories over them."

"No way!" I nearly shout. "She couldn't!"

"Mona Chen has powerful friends in her pocket," Tera reminds me. "Presidents and prime ministers, all desperate to live for ever. You think they wouldn't let her do whatever she wants?"

"So that's why you made those adverts," I realise. "Saying that Pleekas were really good for the environment."

"What?" Tera scowls. "I would never say that!"

"You did! At the G12 Eco-Rally ..."

"The rally ... That happened already?" Tera says, looking dazed. "I can't remember." She rubs her head again. "Look – Anders, is that your name? Where is this car taking us?"

"It's pre-programmed to go to my house," I tell her.

"That's bad." Tera sits up straight. "Chen will work out what's happened when she finds that I've gone and you've vanished too."

I chew my lip, anxious. What have I got myself into? "Uh ... maybe we can tell the police? Get protection?"

"I don't have proof of any of this," says Tera. "Anyway, I told you, New You is above the law. The cops won't touch the foundation. Chen will just send people to bring me back. As for you ..." Tera sighs and shakes her head. "Sorry, Anders, as the old cliché goes – you know too much. That makes you a target for New You too."

"What's Mona going to do to me?" I protest. "She can't lock me up or stop me talking—"

"Of course she can," snaps Tera. "Chen knew that threats could only keep me loyal to New You for so long. So she had a better solution." She looks at me with her cold grey eyes. "She was going to turn me Pleeka."

"Against your will?" I croak. "No way. There are rules. Safeguards."

"Do you believe in the tooth fairy too?" Tera says, leaning forward. "Back at the New You offices, I *saw* it, Anders: a Pleeka me. It was waiting to come to life and take my place. A plastic puppet completely under her control."

# CHAPTER 13

## You Can't Go Home Again

I can't believe what I'm hearing. But Tera's serious about Mona's plans. Dead serious.

"I was strapped down ready," Tera informs me. "Body scanned. Mind copied. Genes cloned. If that power surge hadn't happened when it did—"

My watch starts beeping. It's an incoming call. Panic grips my guts. I tell Tera, "It's my dad."

"If he asks, you haven't seen me," Tera hisses. "Got it?"

I nod and answer the call. Dad's voice sounds in my ear. "Anders? You took the car. Are you all right?"

"Yeah, I ... I just needed to go home. Got freaked by what happened." I'm trying so hard to act normal, but even to my ears I sound fake, fake, fake. "What *did* happen?" I ask.

"Apparently, Jin was affected by an unexplained power surge during a skills download. There was another power surge soon after. It overloaded the company's servers and anything connected to them."

"Like Cody," I realised. "And the float-screens."

"Mona thinks it was a terror attack, but no one's claimed responsibility yet," Dad says. "Cody's all right now. So is Jin. But Mona has postponed the launch until 21:00 hours. In the meantime, Tera Helstrom has disappeared." He pauses. "You didn't see her, did you?"

I swallow hard. "I think I'd remember seeing her, Dad," I tell him.

"Yeah. Well, I'm sure Tera will be back here at New You soon." Dad sounds tired. "Let me know when you get home, OK?"

"Will do. Bye!" I end the call as Tera leans forward to change the destination on the car's float-screen. "Tera, what are you doing?" I ask her.

"I've got to contact my people," she says. "They must be the ones who attacked the New You offices. And if they can disrupt the systems like that once, maybe they can do it again. It'll keep New You off our backs for a bit."

I just nod, in a daze. This is all happening so fast. Part of me wishes I'd never come today. That I was safe at home, happily unaware of what happened at New You.

But a bigger part is thinking, *This is a news story like no other. A story straight from the lips of one of the most famous people in the world.*

*And right now, I have the exclusive.*

\*

Within an hour, Tera and I are standing outside a dusty old antique shop on the edge of London's high-pollution zone. Face masks are meant to be worn here cos the air is bad to breathe. But Tera doesn't bother, so I tell myself it's fine.

I've lent her my hoodie as a disguise because she's so recognisable. All that red hair! She keeps looking down at the pavement as we hurry along cos her grey eyes are still bright and clear despite all she's been through.

Tera lifts a hinged wooden flap at the top of the shop's door frame and takes out an old-fashioned turn-key. I watch her unlock the door and follow her inside.

We've walked quite a way to get here, in case the car can be traced. We don't want it leading Mona straight to Tera's friends.

The shop smells old and is full of antiques: mobile phones and tablets with actual glass screens, DVD players, games consoles. A dark rectangle of plastic with a glowing blue bulb catches my eye. It's the only thing in the whole store that's lit up.

"What's that?" I ponder.

"A wireless router," says Tera, locking the door behind us. "Forty years ago, every home used them to get on the internet. That was before LiFi took over. Me and my friends use them to talk in secret over a private network. Old tech is harder to hack."

"While new tech like Pleekas can be hacked easily," I say. "If you have the right equipment, you can literally mess with people's minds. Edit them. Change them."

"Or sell that power to the government," says Tera, crossing to a door at the back of the shop. "Take someone who's turned Pleeka and decides to join a protest march. If the government don't approve, they can just shut that person down."

I remember how Cody was back at the New You offices: laughing and glitching, unable to reset. She was helpless.

Then I imagine half the population doing the same, and I shudder.

"But everyone's turning themselves into Pleekas," I say. "How can New You be stopped?"

The door ahead of us bursts open, making me gasp. The figure of a man stands in the doorway. The thick smell of engine oil fills the air around him. He steps stiffly into the light, and I see his skin is waxy. Cables trail out from a chunky belt around his waist, snaking out of sight along the

corridor. I hear gears buzz as he turns to look at me. His eyes don't blink.

He's a Pleeka. But he's really basic. More like an old mannequin than a person. Very creepy.

"It's all right," Tera tells me. "This is Shaq. A friend."

"I'm not sure New You *can* be stopped," Shaq says, his voice flat and his eyes unblinking. "Things are worse than we ever imagined."

# CHAPTER 14

## They Know

Shaq moves like an old robot. His legs are stiff and slow as he leads us to a back room in his shop. There's nothing in here except an old TV screen on the wall.

I take a drink from my flask, thirsty from the walk. I offer it to Tera, but she passes.

"Sorry, no chairs," says Shaq. "Pleekas don't need to sit. Just as well, as I haven't been able to bend my legs in years."

"Shaq, this is Anders Jones," Tera says. "He got me out. Works for that cute news show."

Shaq stares at me. "Jones as in Daniel Jones who does *And Finally*?"

"Yeah. That's my dad." I think of the sort of question Dad would ask. "You've been Pleeka a long time, right? Why haven't you upgraded?"

"This version is too basic for New You to thought-control," Shaq explains. "My body might be stuck, but at least my mind is free."

"And so am I," says Tera. "Thanks to you and the Cell."

"The Cell?" I say, feeling uneasy again. "As in, terrorist cell?"

"Terror is what we're up against," says Shaq. "Your news show shines a light on good stuff left in the world, right, Anders? Well, *we* work to protect that good stuff."

"From companies like New You," says Tera. "You said when we arrived you don't think we can stop them, Shaq. What the hell have you found to make you think that?"

"I've not found anything," he says, "but she has." He turns on the screen to show a woman wearing big glasses, sitting at a desk.

"Tera?" the woman on the screen cries. "Oh my god, I can't believe we've got you back!"

"Jenn!" Tera says, jumping up and nearly hugging the screen. "So good to see you …"

I realise I've seen Jenn before. "She was at the Monsta-X press launch," I tell Shaq. "Jenn got thrown out for asking questions Mona couldn't answer."

"But not before she skimmed data from Mona's tech-pass," says Shaq. "Data that helped us break into New You's systems."

"We knew that New You had taken you, Tera," says Jenn. "We just couldn't prove it."

"Well, it was Anders here who got me out of their offices," Tera says, and I feel myself blush. "Anders, meet Jenn. She's a crusader for the truth. Fearless."

"Me, fearless? I'm in hiding," says Jenn. "After I challenged Mona, New You tried to silence me. They've sent me all kinds of threats. I had to drop off the radar."

"What's got them so rattled?" I ask. "What do you know?"

"The truth about the new Pleeka batteries," says Shaq. "We got hold of the design and tested it against *my* old battery, which ran out years ago." He points down at the cables trailing from his waist. "I have to stay plugged in to an electric generator just to keep running."

"The batteries for the Pleekas they're rolling out now do *not* last eighty years like they keep saying," Jenn explains. "They will barely last ten. After that, the cost of replacing them will be so high, only the super-rich will be able to afford them."

I feel cold. "But their old bodies are recycled after three years, so they won't be able to go back ... And there are eight million people turning Pleeka."

"Ten per cent of the UK's population," Shaq agrees. "And with all the publicity, all the high discounts, that's going to rise to at least twenty million people in the next couple of years."

Tera looks horrified. "And when the batteries fail, for most of them it'll be—"

"Lights out," says Jenn. "For ever."

"We have to tell the government," I say. "They're working with New You, pushing everyone to turn Pleeka—"

"The government already know," says Shaq. "They went ahead anyway."

Tera and I look at each other. "You're sure?" she asks Jenn quietly.

"One of my contacts stole a report on the Pleeka Project from the Ministry of Tech," says Jenn. "The order to continue with it was signed by the Prime Minister herself."

"You can see why," says Shaq. "The world's in trouble. There'll be nothing but tough choices ahead for the UK. Getting rid of a quarter of the population can only make things easier."

"Things really are worse than we thought," says Tera grimly. "But there's got to be a way to warn people what's happening."

"My dad's news show," I say. *"And Finally.* It has big ratings. If we cover this story—"

"Your dad's taking money from Mona Chen," Tera retorts. "He won't go against her."

"I bet he will, once he's seen the proof," I say, hoping I'm right. "Do you have copies of this report? Anything I could show him?"

"I made copies," Jenn says.

Then a shadow falls over her.

Someone's there with Jenn in the room.

Jenn looks up and screams. The camera jerks away from the desk with a bang. Blood spatters on a blurry wall, then the screen goes blank.

The three of us are so shocked, we're still staring when we hear banging on the shop's front door.

# CHAPTER 15

## Forced Exit

Tera turns to Shaq, wide-eyed. "That's them at the door, isn't it?" Tera says. "New You."

Shaq grabs me by the shoulders with his mannequin fingers. "You." His face doesn't move, but his voice is angry. "You led them here."

I pull free of his clumsy grip. "I didn't!" I protest.

"He couldn't have led them to Jenn, could he?" Tera says. "Oh, Jenn …"

The banging from the shopfront gets louder.

"The door won't hold long," Shaq says. "Get out of here. The back way."

Tera takes his hand. "What about you?" she asks Shaq.

"Can't exactly run, can I?" Shaq gestures to cables trailing away from his body. "But you ..."

The sound of glass breaking crashes from the main room. Fear jumps in my chest. "Come on!" I hiss, and grab Tera by the arm. I drag her across the room to a door that opens onto a passage. At the end of the passage, there's a glass door.

A blur of shadow on the wall tells me someone is waiting there behind it.

"This way," Tera says. She grabs my hand and almost yanks me off my feet as she runs for the stairs. "Fire escape." She takes them two at a time. Heart pounding, I follow her up onto a dusty landing until we get to a fire door.

Downstairs, I hear a splintering crash. Shaq screams.

Dread fills my stomach like ice-cold water. *How could they have found us so fast?*

As we run towards the fire door, I can guess there'll be someone waiting there. Tera pushes open the door, and I see a guy on the fire escape outside. He's wearing a mask against the smog and holding a gun of some sort.

Tera doesn't stop – she slams into the guy before he has time to fire. The guy falls back against the metal rail of the fire escape. Tera knocks the gun from his hand and knees him in the stomach. He folds over, gasping for breath.

Tera looks back at me. "Move!" she whispers.

I race across the landing and out into the afternoon haze. Tera's already halfway down the fire escape, bounding down the metal steps. I keep both hands on the railings as I bundle down after her. She's already out in the back alley by the time I join her.

"We must get to the main road," says Tera. She shrugs off my hoodie, shaking out her hair. "It's busy there. New You might not grab us if there are enough witnesses to see it …"

I hear a *phut!* of compressed air and feel a scratch at my neck. My fingers stray automatically to the site and come away bloody.

I turn, look up and see another man at the top of the fire escape. I feel a wave of dizziness.

"He got me," I say.

"Tranquiliser or something," says Tera. Again, she drags me after her, charging down the alley to the main road.

We've almost reached the end of the alley when a big silver car swings into sight at speed. Tera's running – she can't stop in time.

My hand slips from hers as I fall to my knees. I see it all, almost in slow motion.

The car smashes into Tera's legs. She rolls onto the bonnet, and her head strikes the windscreen. The glass cracks as she bounces off, thrown like a doll against the alley wall.

I stare at Tera in horror. Not because she's badly injured.

She's not.

Tera gets up. Unharmed. Not a scratch on her.

"You're not the real Tera," I tell her. "You only thought you were." My senses are growing dim and dizzier, but I remember: Tera never drank anything. She looked so fresh. Now I realise what's happened. "Mona turned you Pleeka already," I say, "and you didn't even know …"

That's how Mona's men found us so easily.

*They could track you, Tera. You belong to them ...*

The men are gathered around us now. I know there's no escape.

Tera's staring at me as the tranquiliser takes full effect. It looks like she wants to cry.

But she can't.

# CHAPTER 16

## Waking Up

I wake up, but my eyes stay closed, sticky with sleep. There's a hum of air conditioning that sounds familiar. The slightly perfumed smell in the air is familiar too. I try to move, but my wrists and ankles are strapped down.

Without opening my eyes, I know I'm back at the New You Foundation. Crashing back into my head are memories of Shaq's place and what happened outside, hard and clear. With them comes a stab of fear.

I risk a peek at the room. It's like an operating theatre lined with computer servers. Tera is lying strapped to a high-tech stretcher beside me. Her eyes are open. Of course, cos Pleekas don't need sleep.

"Anders?" Tera says quietly, noticing my movement. "Are you OK?"

"Could be worse," I whisper. "I could be looking at a Pleeka of myself instead of you."

"I wasn't trying to trick you. You know that, right?" Tera says. She shakes her head miserably. "I didn't realise that the body I was looking at was the *real* me and not the Pleeka."

"I can't blame you – I thought you were the real deal too." I lick my dry lips. "You must have been Pleeka when you were promoting New You, under Mona's control. But somehow the real you fought back."

"Back in my right mind," Tera says as she strains against the straps. "But not the right body."

The door opens with a soft swish, and Mona Chen steps in.

"Awake?" she says. "Good." She crosses to stand between me and Tera on our stretchers. "There's no point in struggling. There's no getting away this time. We still have two hours before tonight's Prima Pleeka launch. We'll have you safely back under control before then."

*The launch is at 21:00 hours*, I remember. All we've been through, and it's only taken a few hours. We haven't even upset Mona's timetable.

"What have you done with the real me?" Tera demands. "I want my body back."

"It's been disposed of in our recycling plant," says Mona. "You've seen how lush our gardens are. Blood and bone make an excellent fertiliser."

I flinch and say, "You can't be serious."

"It's a green solution," says Mona. She crosses to a large float-screen in front of the computer servers. "We thought Tera would approve. You've been such a great asset to us, my dear. And with a few more tweaks, you will be again."

"Go to hell," Tera hisses. "You'll never own me. I broke your thought control before. I will again."

"You don't understand," Mona says, almost gently. "The mind is like a storybook told with memories instead of words. Once we take your mind-print, we can edit that story in any way we like. We can change some memories. Remove others."

"Turning a climate activist into a Pleeka-lover was a hell of an edit," I say. "Is that why New

You's version of Tera broke down? Because she *knew* her story didn't make sense? That it was too different from the original?"

Mona nods. "A cancer can be removed by the best surgeons and yet still come back," she says. "But since we have real Tera's original mind-print stored in our server, we can go back to it, edit it again and download it again to her Pleeka body as many times as we have to. We were just about to when your friends started hacking into our systems."

"What happened to Shaq and Jenn?" asks Tera.

Mona shrugs. "I understand they were killed while resisting arrest."

"What were they being arrested for?" I shout. "Knowing too much?"

"The Pleeka Project is too important to risk any bad publicity," says Mona.

"So what happens to me?" I ask, feeling sick. "You going to 'remove' me too?"

"Come now, Anders," Mona says. "We don't want your father upset. He's so useful to us." Mona goes on changing settings on the screen. "We'll just have to make you a Pleeka too."

"No!" The word jumps from my mouth.

"It's the best way to erase those troublesome memories."

"You can't force me!" I say, closing my eyes. I don't want to end up like poor Tera. "You think my dad won't be upset if you turn me into a robot?"

Mona looks at me, her eyes curious. "You're really convinced that Pleekas are evil, aren't you?" she says, crossing to my stretcher. "Human progress has changed the world. Now we must change with it – or face extinction. Pleekas are the only hope for human survival. Don't you see? Pleekas don't need clean water. Pleekas don't need clean air to breathe. Pleekas can survive nuclear radiation …"

Tera snorts. "Drop a bomb on one," she says, "and it still goes bang."

"The host body might. But the mind is kept safely in the Cloud. It can be downloaded into another body at any time," says Mona. "The ultimate survival tool."

"Everyone lives for ever so long as they can afford it," I say. "So long as they're approved of by New You and the government, right? Well, if it's so good to be Pleeka, how come you're not one yourself?"

"But I *am* a Pleeka, Anders," Mona replies. She places her hand on my shoulder and squeezes, so hard it feels like the bone will break. As I gasp with pain, her perfect smile grows wider. "I am ready for the future that humans have created."

# CHAPTER 17

## Gamble

I can't believe Mona is a Pleeka. I stare up at her, panting for breath and wishing I could rub my sore shoulder, and I can't see any telltale signs. There are little blemishes on her skin. One eye is a bit bloodshot. Her forehead is marked with frown lines.

Mona looks completely real.

"I guess you're the top-of-the-range model," says Tera. "A walking advert for Pleekas."

"A perfect copy of the original," Mona agrees. "That is a strong draw for the rich and powerful."

"Like the prime minister, you mean?" Tera sneers. "Your friends and funders in government?"

"Our plans for the UK are just a first step," says Mona. "Bigger countries with larger populations will be watching. China. Japan. The United States ..."

"Billions of Pleekas," I realise. "But the raw materials needed to make those ..."

"They'll cost the Earth," says Tera. "Literally."

"Really, Tera, turn that frown upside down," Mona says. She's smiling again. "In two hours from now, you'll be telling everybody how vital it is that young people become Pleekas to help save the world."

Tera grimaces.

"The launch for Prima Pleekas will show the world that everything is still on track," says Mona. "Cody has fully recovered. Monsta-X will perform without a hitch. And you'll be right back on our side, Tera, once your edited mind-print has been downloaded." Mona crosses back to the float-screen. "Let's see to that now, shall we?"

"It's not going to work!" Tera shouts. "I'm as stubborn as hell. It's not gonna work!"

As she speaks, I feel my insides jump.

Those words.

Jin from Monsta-X had said those exact words after trying to download his dance moves when they'd been muddled by Shaq's attack on the server.

"*It's not gonna work!*" Cody had said that too, not long after she'd tried to download something from the New You servers.

Both of them had glitched and spoken Tera's words. It was almost as if Tera's old, human mind-print had got stuck in the system like a digital ghost and was shouting for help.

What if it was still there, waiting for a way out through another Pleeka?

What if Tera's digital ghost could make it into Mona's mind? It could mess with her head and make her glitch, like Jin and Cody. It might even screw up the New You launch for the second time today.

It was worth a try. What did I have to lose? If I could only get Mona to download something …

"My dad," I call. "How are you gonna explain me ending up a Pleeka?"

"It's a simple matter to arrange an accident in an auto-cab," says Mona. "We'll say you'd have died from your injuries unless we turned you Pleeka. Of course, you'll have to be placed in a generic youth body at first. But I'm sure your father will pay for upgrades so it looks more like the old you."

She's so casual about it all. I feel panic firing up inside me, but I try to focus. "You don't get it, Mona," I say. "Dad's only been pretending to work for you. He's been gathering evidence about the New You Foundation all along!"

Mona swings round to look at me. "That's a pathetic lie, Anders," she says coolly.

"I'm not lying," I insist. "Dad's been playing you. He only took your money so he could snoop on your business more easily."

"Anders!" Tera shouts. "How can you do this to your dad?" She sounds shocked. Good. That might help to convince Mona. And I need to convince her if my plan is going to work.

"Mona, I'll prove it," I tell her. "Let me go, and I'll give you access to Dad's data cloud. I mean, I don't know where he's keeping the evidence, but hopefully—"

"How convenient," says Mona. I can see she's still suspicious. "Well, I'll just copy all of his data to our server and go through it at my leisure. If your father is really so foolish as to cross us ..." Mona frees one of my wrists. "Unlock your smartwatch."

I look her in the eyes. "Promise you won't turn me Pleeka?" I say.

"Promise," she replies.

I hesitate. There's tons of data in our cloud. What if Mona gets someone else to go through it all? If she doesn't download anything herself, there's no chance of Tera's digital mind-print reaching her.

But I'm out of options. I have no other plans.

"All right," I say.

I look into my watch to unlock it, then log in to Dad's cloud. It's lucky the real Tera can't reach me. She looks like she wants to tear my head off.

"You can't trust New You!" Tera shouts. "You know what Mona's done."

I want to tell her, *It's OK. This is a trick. There* is *no evidence. And if the real you is still hiding in that download connection, she can zip straight into Mona's head. Right?*

Mona takes my watch in one hand and opens a float-screen with the other. She starts swiping all Dad's data across to the New You server.

Once she's finished, I speak again. "I think the evidence is in an audio file," I tell her. "But since you're a Pleeka, I guess you can download all recordings direct to your head."

"Anders!" Tera bellows. "No!"

My heartbeat races cos Mona's eyes are closed, the eyeballs beneath rolling. It looks like she's downloading already! I can hear a faint humming as she receives the data.

*Glitch*, I think desperately. *Start glitching ...*

But then her eyes open. Mona is fine. She's frowning.

"There it is," she says. "Your father's evidence against us. Just as you said."

I feel sick. My mouth goes dry.

*No way*, I'm thinking.

I was actually *right?*

Dad really *was* playing New You for suckers all along?

"There are phone calls," Mona says. "Secret recordings. Interviews with former staff. Profiles of those Pleeka miners trapped on the seabed ..." Mona closes her eyes, still humming as she scans the data. "Your father's smarter than I thought. This might really have finished the company."

I close my eyes. I've blown it. Blown everything.

Mona will kill the story.

And she'll kill me and Dad with it.

# CHAPTER 18

## Switch

Five minutes later, I'm being marched away from Mona's medical lab by two security guards. Mona told them to take me to an auto-cab while she arranged to have Dad picked up from the studio. He's there waiting for the launch to start. I guess the two of us will be back together real soon.

I'm too numb even to cry. I can't believe how badly my plan has backfired. Mona has no reason to make me a Pleeka any more. No reason to keep Dad sweet now she knows he was out to expose her.

I've ruined everything. I'm dead. Dad's dead.

That accident Mona was going to fake for me is going to be for real.

They escort me along empty corridors. They're the same ones I took with Tera when I helped her get out of here. There's no chance of running into anyone who might help.

Ugh. I can't believe how badly I've messed up. Why couldn't Dad have told me what he was doing? I thought he was taking cash from New You to help push Pleekas. Really, he was working to reveal their lies. How was I to know that my attempt to trip up Mona would ruin everything?

I can feel tears prickling behind my eyes. But I can't afford to go to pieces now.

The guards open a back door, and we're out in the grounds. Night is falling. We round a corner of the building, and I see an auto-cab waiting with its headlights on. My stomach twists as I realise Dad is standing next to it, arguing with a woman from security.

"I'm not leaving," Dad says. He waves his camera in her face. "See this? An hour from now I'm supposed to record Mona's press call for my news show. It's an automatic satellite link-up. Worldwide connection."

"Your pass is no longer valid," the woman says. She notices me and the guards. "You and your son will be escorted from the grounds."

"Anders?" Dad says, and looks across at me. He's so confused. "I thought you were at home. What are you doing here?"

I don't know what to say. The woman pushes Dad into the back of the auto-cab, then walks to the main building, leaving my two security guards to take care of things.

One of them opens the other back door and shoves me inside. He asks his mate, "Got the auto-cab destination code?"

"Downloading it now," he says. He crosses to the front of the car and leans in through the window to tap the data into the auto-driver.

"Dad," I whisper, "I'm so sorry. I've messed up everything."

Dad stares. "Anders, what is it?" he asks.

"Mona knows," I tell him. "They know what you've been doing. Pretending to help." Breathless, I pour out a confused version of events while Dad becomes steadily more horrified.

"And now they're going to kill us in a fake accident!" I finish, wiping my eyes.

"It's not gonna work," says the guard, still staring at the auto-driver.

"What do you mean, it's not gonna work?" the other guard asks. He walks round the car to join his mate.

I spot a red disc sticking out from his back pocket.

*A sleep-switch*, I realise. Mona used one on Jin when he had his fit. What did she say? *"It safely powers down the brain into sleep mode."* After what happened today, maybe all the guards carry them.

"It's not gonna work," the first guard says. "I'm stubborn ... stubborn ..." He starts to shake.

Dad lifts his camera and starts recording the action. The guard reaches into his back pocket for the sleep-switch, and I jump out of the car. I run round and snatch the red disc from his hand. Taken by surprise, the guard turns – and I slap the disc against his forehead. He grunts, lunges for me – and falls flat on his face.

"Anders!" Dad shouts. He looks shocked but also kind of impressed. "Quick – the other guard."

I put the disc to his forehead too. The second guard goes rigid, then falls away from the car.

Dad is already tapping at the auto-driver. "Come on," he says. "I think you stopped him before he could set this thing to crash. And we need to get out of here."

"No, Dad, wait," I tell him. "What happened just now to the guard. I don't know how, but it's Tera. A ghost of her, passing into other Pleekas, messing them up."

"It's bought us time to get away," Dad says. "We need time to work out what we—"

"There *is* no time," I tell him. "I thought we could mess up Mona in the same way, but I guess she's too advanced. She's trying to turn Tera into her pet Pleeka, and if I can stop it …"

"I can't let you go back in there," Dad says. "You're just—"

"A news reporter, like you," I interrupt. "Dad, you've got your camera. You're clear to broadcast live at 21:00. The whole world will be able to watch whatever we show them."

"What *can* we show them?" Dad says. "The evidence in our cloud isn't edited. The story's not ready. I've been building a case against the New You Foundation for months. Taking their bribes, covering the stories they wanted me to, getting closer—"

"Yeah, and I wish you'd told me," I say. "Why didn't you?"

"You know how dangerous these people are," Dad says. "I didn't dare tell you. I didn't want you involved."

"Well, I *am* involved," I shoot back. "And so is Tera." I point to the main building. "She's in there. If we can get her out, we'll have all the evidence we need!"

# CHAPTER 19

## Break-In Point

Me and Dad are hiding out in the bushes in the grounds. We've circled the building looking for the best way in. There isn't one. All I've spotted are two small windows left open on the ground floor.

I feel sick when I think of Tera's real body being recycled and fed into the soil here, while the Pleeka version of Tera is just a puppet to parade at a Pleeka press launch.

Dad sent the auto-cab away so Mona would think we'd been driven off as planned. But how long do we have before Mona finds out the "accident" hasn't happened? How long before those two security guards are missed – or wake up and come looking for us?

It's Mona's press launch in just ten minutes.

"What are we going to do?" I whisper.

"Get back inside through that first window you saw," says Dad. "It's closest to the studio, and that's where Tera will be taken. Perhaps you'll get a chance to reach her."

"Perhaps," I breathe. "But you won't fit through that window, Dad."

"True. So while you squeeze inside, I'll let the security guards spot me in the grounds," Dad says. "If they're busy chasing after me, you'll stand a better chance of getting about undetected." He hands me his camera. "With this."

I give Dad a crooked smile. "Breaking in. Filming illegally," I say. "You realise this is terrible parenting."

"You're not a kid," says Dad, a bit gruffly. "You're a reporter. If the studio is too well guarded, try to get back to that lab. You might find some evidence of what they've done to Tera."

"I'll try," I say. I look at him and think of all the fun times we've had together on *And Finally*.

With Mum, and then just the two of us after she died. Making news, making stories.

How is this story going to end?

"Remember, the camera feed will go live at nine," says Dad. "If you can't do anything else, broadcast a message asking for help. Tell the world what New You are doing. Share your story."

"Mona will just say it's a hoax," I argue. "She'll fake evidence against *us*."

"Probably," says Dad. "But it might still get other people asking their own questions." He rests a hand on my shoulder.

For a few grateful seconds, I take the comfort of his touch.

Then, with a last smile, Dad dives out from the bushes and runs across the lawn.

I don't watch his progress. I don't dare. I just creep away through the bushes, making for the window.

I wrestle Dad's camera into my hoodie pocket and then dart across to the building. I manage to open the window wide enough for me to squeeze inside.

I'm in a meeting room. Expensive leather chairs are arranged around a long wooden table. As I open the door onto an empty corridor, my heart is thumping. I grip the red sleep-switch in my right hand and tap Dad's camera to be sure it's still in my pocket. Imagine if I *can* get evidence of what Mona did to Tera and broadcast *that* alongside New You's press launch ...

For a minute, I almost believe that I can do this.

But as I make my way along the corridor, I hear the murmur of voices behind a door. I recognise two of the voices – they belong to Cody Vempati and her mother. The door is marked "Green Room". A green room is a place where the "talent" sits before making their big appearance on stage or in a studio.

I want to warn Cody that her perfect Pleeka body is anything but perfect. But I know that if I show my face in there, I'll be grabbed by security guards straight away.

Suddenly, I hear footsteps from behind a corner. I turn, frantic. I need to get out of sight.

Too late.

Tera walks into sight.

"Anders!" she exclaims. She runs up to me, all smiles.

I almost laugh with relief. "You're all right! You got away!"

Tera's smile fades. "No," she says. "I didn't."

Suddenly, she grabs my arm. And I realise: *Tera must be back under Mona's control.*

"I heard you escaped," she says, pushing me against the wall. "I've been looking for you."

"Tera, please," I hiss. "Let me go."

"I can't." She tugs Dad's camera out of my hoodie pocket.

"Give that back," I beg her. "Tera, please. Without that camera—"

"Shut up, Anders," Tera says, her perfect grey eyes fixing on to mine. "The press launch *will* go ahead."

# CHAPTER 20

## Ghost in the Machine

Tera opens the door and pushes me inside the green room. On the far side, there's another door that leads into the studio. A small crowd of people are filing through it now, taking their seats for the press conference. Cody and her mum glance back at me just before they leave the green room. I watch as they take seats in the front row of the studio. Mona Chen's well-groomed assistant escorts Jin from Monsta-X to a seat beside them. He looks fine now. Like nothing ever happened.

Mona Chen is preparing to go through to the studio too. She's checking over notes with three men in grey suits while a security guard stands watch. The guard sees me with Tera. He runs over and grabs me.

Now Mona looks up and notices I'm here. I wait for her triumphant smile to smear itself over her face. But she just stares coldly.

"About time, Tera," Mona says.

"Sorry," Tera says, holding up my camera as she walks over. "I had to make sure we got this."

"Very good," says Mona. "Now, my fellow directors, we'd better join our friends in the studio."

The guys in suits nod. "Ready for the big moment," one of them says. Then he turns to my guard. "Keep the boy here and make sure the perimeter is locked down," he orders. "Post more guards on all entrances. If his father tries to disrupt the launch ... Well, you know what to do."

From the serious looks on everyone's faces, I reckon it's not "throw a party".

I watch the last of the crowd enter the studio. The New You directors sit beside Cody's mother in the front row. Cody, Jin and Tera are sitting at the side of the stage area. Mona walks to a podium at the front of the stage, cool and calm as if nothing has happened.

"What are you going to do to me?" I ask the guard.

"Finish what was started," he replies, staring through the window into the studio. "Now, shut up."

There doesn't seem much more to say anyway.

Two minutes later, it's 21:00. Dramatic music starts to play. A virtual banner proclaiming that "Age Is Just a Number" appears above the stage as lights sweep all around the studio. Fake applause begins.

Mona smiles and nods to the camera. "Welcome to you all," she declares. "An estimated two billion of you are watching live!"

I close my eyes. The *And Finally* broadcast should be going out now. *Sorry, Dad*, I think miserably. *I let you down.*

"Tonight, we launch the Prima Pleeka programme," says Mona. "We have millions of sixteen-year-olds on our waiting list, ready to swap tired old flesh and blood for shiny, perfect bio-plastic. But before we hear from our very first Prima Pleeka, Cody Vem ... Vem ... Vem ..."

My eyes snap open. Mona's voice is glitching. She can't say Cody's surname.

Her head judders on her elegant neck. "Before we hear from her," Mona says, "I must tell you the truth about the Pleeka Project."

I'm holding my breath. What's going on? Through the window I can see Cody's mum frowning. The directors in the front row are swapping nervous looks.

Mona continues: "With the full support of the British government, the New You Foundation has been tricking the public into becoming Pleekas, offering them cash incentives and false claims ..."

My god. Things are really kicking off now. Forms signed by the Prime Minister appear on the screen ... then pictures of Mona and the suited men cosying up with the Prime Minister and the Minister for Climate ... then a report on failed battery tests.

"A Pleeka power source will last barely *ten* years before it must be renewed," says Mona.

"What?" Cody's mum gasps.

I don't understand what's happening either. These revelations will destroy the New You Foundation. Why is Mona Chen fessing up now?

One of the directors jumps to his feet and runs to the window. He gestures wildly to the guard to come into the studio. The guard runs over to the door, dragging me with him.

"The Prime Minister has agreed that renewing a battery will cost more than even wealthy citizens can afford," Mona is saying. "Those who cannot pay will become AI only, existing only in the Cloud with no further influence in the real world …"

As the guard opens the door, I twist free. I push into the studio and slam the door shut on his arm. He shouts with pain, so I guess he's no Pleeka. He yanks his arm free of the door and reels backwards.

My heart's in my mouth. The screen behind Mona is showing police body-cam footage of what happened today: Shaq recoiling as his cables are pulled out. Poor Jenn being shot dead at her desk.

"Some people have tried to expose our plans. They have been executed," says Mona calmly. "The New You Board of Directors are guilty of murder and of conspiracy to murder. We have left a team of six underwater miners to a living death, trapped in an abyss in the ocean."

I watch pictures of the miners come up on screen, as they were before they were trapped down in the dark depths for ever. Smiling. Proud.

"Shut her down!" yells one of the suited men. He tries to pull Mona away from the podium, but Jin from Monsta-X springs forward in a flying jump kick.

"I'm stubborn as hell!" Jin shouts. Just like he did this afternoon. His foot connects with the suited man's chin, sending him sprawling into his fellow director.

Mona continues: "The Prime Minister herself has signed off on a policy allowing New You to alter the mind of anyone protesting against government policy …"

The studio is becoming a confused free-for-all. Another security guard tries to grab Mona. I hurl myself at him in a clumsy rugby tackle and manage to bring him down. He grabs me in a neck-lock. I gasp for breath.

"It's not gonna work," says Cody Vempati as she drags the guard off me with superhuman strength. As I stand up, the guard whose arm I hurt tries to push me over. Mrs Vempati comes to help me, pushing him away.

"The New You Foundation abducted Tera Helstrom and have kept her captive for five weeks," Mona goes on. "Tera's endorsements of Pleekas were false and given under duress ..."

"You're finished, Chen!" shouts one of the suited directors. "Whatever you're playing at, it was for nothing. We ended transmission the second you went off script."

"Then how come she's all over the internet?" says another director, jabbing at the screen on his smartwatch. "There are calls to ban Pleekas and arrest all of us. Calls for riots against the government ..."

Then I see Tera, still sitting at the side of the stage.

She's holding my dad's camera. Filming everything.

They forgot about *And Finally*. Forgot about our satellite upload that let us show all the footage live.

The truth of all of this is out in the world now.

More security guards come into the room. Jin and Cody work together, fighting them off so Mona can go on confessing. The Pleeka guard who started glitching in the auto-cab has turned on his fellow guards too. People are brawling and sprawling all over the studio.

I make my way over to Tera. She sets down the camera, leaves it recording and shelters with me at the back of the room.

"What the hell happened?" I ask her. "Is that you? The real you?"

"As real as it gets," Tera says. "My original mind-print was being held in the New You systems. Shaq's hack-attack released it. Any data downloaded by a Pleeka got a digital stowaway. Me!"

"So you *did* get inside Jin and Cody," I realise. "And you got into Mona!"

Tera smiles. "Living rent-free in her head," she says. "When the time was right, I took control of her Pleeka. Thanks to you, she'd downloaded your dad's evidence and a ton more besides, meaning I was able to put it on screen."

Thanks to me? I almost collapse with relief. I thought I'd ruined everything.

"I know your download trick didn't work as you planned it, Anders," Tera goes on. "But it really was a brilliant move."

"Get out of my head," I tease her. "But you're still in Cody's and Jin's head's too, aren't you? And the guard as well. You're in every Pleeka who's downloaded something from the server!"

"Told you I'm stubborn. Not even a sleep-switch gets rid of my digital stowaway," Tera agrees. "There's strength in numbers, right? Now, come on, we're reaching the end of your broadcast ..."

I look out over the mayhem in the room. Mona is standing silent, her evidence given. The directors are screaming at each other. They look sick. Shocked. They know they're finished.

I cross to my dad's camera and crouch down in front of it. "For *And Finally*, this is Anders Jones saying goodnight to the New You Foundation and everyone who supports them. And good riddance to you all."

# CHAPTER 21

## Age Is Just a Number

Things didn't change overnight, but it didn't take long.

Let me tell you what happened.

Tera used Mona to call the police to the New You offices. Mona told them her security forces had turned against her. The police turned up and arrested the guards before Dad could be caught. He followed the police into the building to find me.

Dad found a whole lot more than that going on, of course! Me and Tera slipped away in all the confusion.

Back home, we found that the *And Finally* footage had gone totally viral and way beyond the UK alone. The next day, people turned out in force – both humans and Pleekas – to protest against the government. The United Nations got involved, accusing Britain's rulers of committing atrocities against its own people. Mona Chen was arrested as soon as she was rebooted, along with the New You Foundation's board of directors.

My dad and I filmed Mona and the directors as they were led from their building into a convoy of police cars. Protestors booed and jeered them. It was the sweetest story I think we've ever run.

Of course, there are a hell of a lot of Pleekas still around – Cody and Jin, and a million more. Most are waiting to be put back into their old bodies. But Tera hasn't got one, and nor do many others who've been Pleeka for more than three years. Their bodies have been recycled.

Always the activist, Tera has become the spokesperson for the Pleeka victims. Who better to stand up for Pleeka rights? They're suing New You for damages. The money they are likely to win will keep them in new batteries for a long time, and new, built-in firewalls will protect their minds from outside attack. Maybe one day Pleekas will be able to run on solar power or other green energies. But experts think it will take a long time before people are willing to trust replica bodies again.

In the meantime, it seems we'll have to find other solutions to the problems of living today. Don't get me wrong, there's still hope in the world. Still happy little stories for me and Dad to cover. But we're reporting on bigger stories too. We're helping to make sure the big tech giants and energy companies stay in line. That they give back to the environment as well as take from it. There are still wins. There *is* still hope.

I just wish I could roll back time to the 2020s, or even the 2030s, when there was a better chance to change things.

Of course, as the years go by, I'll get older. Tera won't. She'll stay the same into the next century and beyond. The same energy. The same anger. The same hard wish to make things right.

We can all hold on to that. Whatever body we're in.

Our books are tested
for children and young people by
children and young people.

Thanks to everyone who consulted on
a manuscript for their time and effort in
helping us to make our books better
for our readers.